Designed by Christine Jaszkowiak

No part of this publication may be reproduced or stored
in a retrieval system, or transmitted in any form or by any means, electronic,
mechanical, photocopying, recording, or otherwise, without written permission
of the publisher. For information regarding permission, write to
Disney Licensed Publishing, 500 S. Buena Vista St., Burbank, CA 91521.

Copyright © 2005 by Disney Enterprises, Inc./Pixar Animation Studios

Published by Scholastic Inc., 557 Broadway, New York, NY 10012,
by arrangement with Disney Licensed Publishing.
SCHOLASTIC, UNDERSEA SCHOOL, and associated logos are trademarks
and/or registered trademarks of Scholastic Inc.

ISBN 0-439-79885-X

12 11 10 9 8 7 6 5 4 3 2 1   5 6 7 8 9 10/0

Printed in the U.S.A.
First Scholastic printing, May 2005

Disney · PIXAR

FINDING NEMO

UNDERSEA SCHOOL

Star Student

by Annie Auerbach

Illustrated by Philip Hom, Hom & Hom Illustration, and John Loter

SCHOLASTIC INC.

New York • Toronto • London • Auckland • Sydney
Mexico City • New Delhi • Hong Kong • Buenos Aires

PARK PUBLIC SCHOOL
6 HYDE PARK DRIVE
GEORGETOWN, ONTARIO   L7G 2B

Nemo loved school. Each morning, he would wake up early and get ready for school. He made sure to brush himself against his anemone home before his father, Marlin, took him to the school yard.

"Ready?" Marlin asked his son.
"Yes!" replied Nemo. "Let's go!"

Nemo was a very curious clown fish. He was always asking his father tons of questions. "Sandy Plankton said that some fish only swim backwards. Is that true? And Sandy Plankton also said that if you touch a pebble to a shark's tail it will turn into a sea star. And Sandy Plankton—"

"I don't know if I want you hanging around Sandy Plankton so much," Marlin said teasingly.

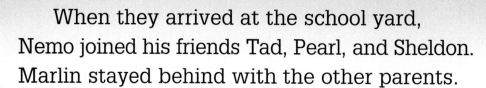

When they arrived at the school yard,
Nemo joined his friends Tad, Pearl, and Sheldon.
Marlin stayed behind with the other parents.

"'Bye, Dad!" Nemo called and swam to get a ride on Mr. Ray, the science teacher.

During his class, Mr. Ray made an announcement: "It's time for the Star Student contest!"

Everyone swam around excitedly. The Star Student contest determined who was the best all-around student.

"*I'm* going to win!" declared Tad.
I wonder if I'm good enough to win,
Nemo thought to himself.

For the first part of the contest, Mr. Ray asked each student a question about science.

He called on Pearl first. "What kind of reef are we in?"

"Uh…a coral reef?" answered Pearl.

"That's right!" Mr. Ray said, and Pearl twirled around happily.

Then he called on Nemo. "What is the name of the place where you live?"

Nemo knew that! "It's called an anennomene, an ennonome, an—"

Mr. Ray stopped him. "I think you're trying to say 'an anemone.' And that's right!" he said.

Nemo nodded, but he was a little disappointed that he couldn't say the word himself.

13

Next was music class. To get points for the Star Student contest, each student had to play his or her instrument.

Pearl clapped her sand dollar cymbals together.
Tad strummed his seaweed harp. And Sheldon
drummed up some music with a
few baby clams.

But when
Nemo blew
as hard as
he could into
a shell horn, it
wasn't music to
anyone's ears!

Nemo felt sad. "I'm not very good at anything," he said. "I don't have any chance of being the Star Student."

"That's not true," said Pearl. "There's still time. Anyone could win."

Sheldon agreed. "Besides, everyone's good at different things."

"Thanks, guys," said Nemo with a half smile.

Soon Nemo and his friends headed for their
exercise class with a special guest teacher, Dory.

"You have one minute to swim around the coral,"
explained Dory. "Whoever swims the fastest wins
points toward the Star Student contest...at least I
think that's what the rules are."

Dory was a fun teacher, but her memory wasn't
the greatest!

ZOOM! All the fish took off and raced around and around. At the finish, Tad was the fastest. Nemo did his best, but his "lucky" fin made it a little harder for him to swim.

As Tad was celebrating his victory, something terrible happened. . . .

Just beyond the school yard, Sandy Plankton
got caught in a giant clam!

"Oh no!" cried Pearl.

"What are we going to do?" asked Sheldon.

"Mfmmftt!" yelled Sandy Plankton.

Suddenly, Nemo had a great idea. "Follow me!" he called to the others.

They raced off and followed Nemo to the lunchroom where they all gathered up some food.

They returned to the giant clam, and Nemo whispered to the others, "Just do what I do." Then he took some algae in his fins. He bravely approached the clam. "Uh, hey, Mr. Clam, would you like a piece of my algae? It's much more tasty than that fish you have."

Tad joined in. "Or some of my kelp sandwich? It's so yummy!" he said and licked his lips.

Nemo hoped his offer to trade would work. Soon, the giant clam opened his mouth to try the tasty sandwich…and Sandy swam out!

Nemo's plan worked! Sandy was free!

Just then, Mr. Ray rushed over. "What are you all doing out here?" he asked. "What happened?"

Nemo's friends were only too happy to tell Mr. Ray. "Nemo saved Sandy!" they cheered.

"You're the bravest fish I know," Pearl told Nemo.

"Aw, it was no big deal," said Nemo, grinning.

But Nemo's friends thought it *was* a big deal. In fact, they all decided to drop out of the Star Student contest so Nemo would win.

"But why?" Nemo asked. "I'm not the best at music, or swimming, or—"

"You're the best at being a friend," Sheldon told him.

26

Everyone heartily agreed.
Soon, Nemo was presented with
the Star Student award and a
bag of seaweed sweets.

"Thanks, everyone," said
Nemo, "but there's only one
way that I'll accept
this award."

"What's that?" Tad asked.

"If you'll all share the sweets with me!" Nemo said. "Besides, what's the fun in winning if I can't share it with all my friends?"

And that's just what they did!

The End

29